To Beth, who liked hospital

First published in hardback in Great Britain by Andersen Press Ltd in 2000
First published in paperback by Collins Picture Books in 2001
3 5 7 9 10 8 6 4
ISBN: 0-00-710957-1
Collins Picture Books is an imprint of the Children's Division, part of HarperCollins Publishers Ltd.
Text and illustrations copyright © Tony Ross 2000, 2001
The author/illustrator asserts the moral right to be identified as the author/illustrator of the work.
A CIP catalogue record for this title is available from the British Library.

The HarperCollins website address is: www.harpercollinschildrensbooks.co.uk
Printed in Hong Kong

I Don't Want To Go To Hospital

Tony Ross

HarperCollins *Children's Books*

"Ooo, Oww, Ooo," cried the Little Princess.
"My nose hurts!"

"You've got a little lump up there," said the Doctor.

"I'll get it out," said the General, drawing his sword.

"No," said the Doctor, "it won't come out. Her Majesty must go to hospital."

"No!" cried the Princess. "I don't want to go to hospital!"

"It's nice in hospital," said the Doctor. "You'll get sweets and cards."

"I don't want to go," said the Princess.

"It's nice in hospital," said the Queen, who had been there.
"I don't want to go," said the Princess.

"You'll meet lots of new friends in hospital," said the Prime Minister.

"No! I don't *want* to go to hospital," said the Princess, and she ran out of the room.

"Where is the Princess?" cried the Queen. "It's time to go."

"She's not in her room," said the Maid.

"She's not in the dustbin," said the Cook.

"She's not in any of my boats," said the Admiral.

"She's not on the roof," said the Gardener.

"She's in the attic!" said the King.
"I don't want to go to hospital," said the Princess.

But the Little Princess had to go.

And the lump came out of her nose.

"Now you are better," said the Queen, "you can brush your teeth, and comb your hair...

...and tidy your room, and..."
"No!" cried the Princess...

"... I want my tonsils out!"

"But why?" said the Queen.
"I want to go back to hospital," said the Little Princess.

"They treated me like a Princess in there."

Collect all the funny stories featuring the demanding Little Princess!

"The Little Princess has huge appeal to toddlers and Tony Ross's illustrations are brilliantly witty."
Practical Parenting

I Want My Potty — *Tony Ross* — 0-00-662687-4

I Want To Be — *Tony Ross* — 0-00-664357-4

I Want My Dinner — *Tony Ross* — 0-00-664356-6

I Want A Sister — *Tony Ross* — 0-00-664730-8

I Don't Want To Go To Hospital — *Tony Ross* — 0-00-710957-1

Tony Ross was born in London in 1938. His dream was to work with horses but instead he went to art college in Liverpool. Since then, Tony has worked as an art director at an advertising agency, a graphic designer, a cartoonist, a teacher and a film maker – as well as illustrating over 250 books! Tony, his wife Zoe and family live in Macclesfield, Cheshire.